DisNEy GiRLS

Cinderella's Castle

Gabrielle Charbonnet

DISNEY PRESS

N E W   Y O R K

Printed in the United States of America.

First Edition

1 3 5 7 9 10 8 6 4 2

The text of this book is set in 15-point Adobe Garamond.

Library of Congress Catalog Card Number: 98-84794

ISBN: 0-7868-4165-6

For more Disney Press fun, visit www.DisneyBooks.com

Contents

CHAPTER 1   Cinderella's Dream   1

CHAPTER 2   Party!   7

CHAPTER 3   My Best Friend Is a Princess   11

CHAPTER 4   A New Me   17

CHAPTER 5   The Transformation Continues   23

CHAPTER 6   Cinderella's Castle   27

CHAPTER 7   Castle Panic   33

CHAPTER 8   Disney Girls to the Rescue!   39

CHAPTER 9   The Last Straw   44

CHAPTER 10   Princesses Just Want to Have Fun   51

CHAPTER 11   One Step Forward, Two Steps Back   60

CHAPTER 12   Help, Disney Girls!   65

CHAPTER 13   Complete Castle Meltdown   71

CHAPTER 14   A Dream Come True   77

Disney Girls

Cinderella's Castle

Chapter One

Cinderella's Dream

Seven-thirty: The Princess arises.

I opened my eyes and blearily shut off my alarm clock. No little bluebirds were fluttering around me, waiting to help me make my bed.

Seven thirty-five: The Princess attends to her pet mice.

Still in my long flannel nightgown, I padded across my room. I measured out some mouse chow and opened the lid of the cage. My two pet mice, Jaq and Gus, squeaked eagerly, the way they do every morning. As I filled their small dish, their pink noses wiggled and their whiskers twitched. They're so cute! I rubbed my finger down their silky little backs. They started munching as I unfastened their water bottle to refill it.

Seven forty-three: The Princess gets dressed.

I opened my closet door. You would think a princess would have a ton of cool clothes, but my clothes are so *not*. No matter how much I stood there staring at my closet, nothing jumped out at me, saying, "Wear me! I'm a cute outfit!"

I sighed and brushed my bed-hairdo out of my eyes. Slowly, a very faint sound of music came to me. It sounded like a waltz. I closed my eyes and . . . there it was! Yes! Magic, right here in my room!

My skin tingled, and I opened my eyes to see my room grow darker except for one corner that glowed with a shimmery blue light. I watched amazed as the blue light changed into . . . my fairy godmother!

"Good morning, my dear," she said in a kind voice.

"Good morning," I managed to get out. My own fairy godmother! I mean, I always knew I had one (everyone does), but I had never seen her before. Wow! What a way to start a Friday morning!

"Heavens," she said, looking at me. "You can't go to school like that."

I looked down at my nightgown and shook my head. Everyone in my third grade class would probably fall on the ground laughing if I showed up in this.

My fairy godmother found her magic wand and waved it. Tiny electric sparkles of magic glittered. Then I felt kind of glowy and warm, as if I were standing in the sun. I blinked, and when I looked down, I was wearing the most adorable outfit: a short, pleated, red plaid skirt, topped by a long-sleeved, fuzzy green sweater. A green velvet headband held my sandy-blond hair back. I stared at myself in the mirror, awed by my transformation. I looked totally cool—like a real princess at last!

"Oh, thank you, fairy godmother—" I began, but was interrupted by a knock on my door. Poof! My fairy god-mother disappeared. Her glowy blue light disappeared. My door opened, and my stepsister Lucy stuck her head into my room. Panicked, I glanced down at myself. Yep. The magic was over. I was back in my faded flannel nightgown.

"Ella," said Lucy impatiently. "Hurry up. It's after eight. It's your turn to unload the dishwasher."

"Sorry," I muttered. "I'll be right down."

Lucy snorted and closed the door. I turned back to my open closet and stared at my clothes again. Same old lame clothes. I sighed, feeling more like myself than ever.

Myself means me, Cinderella. Yep, *that* Cinderella. My name is Ella O'Connor. For practically my whole life, my dad and I shared a small, cozy apartment here in Willow Hill, which is a suburb of Orlando, Florida. (My mom died when I was only two years old. I don't remember her, but I love seeing pictures of her. She was really pretty.)

Then last July, Dad got married again, to a woman named Alana Rogers. She's my stepmother. She has two daughters of her own: Jane, who's twelve, and in seventh grade at Orlando Middle School; and Lucy, who's fourteen, and in ninth grade at Orlando High. So now I have a stepmother and two stepsisters. Sounds familiar, right?

The five of us moved into a house (still in Willow Hill—yay!) right after the wedding. I like our new house okay, but it's less cozy than our apartment was. My new room is great, though. It's big and sunny, in the front of the house, and it has a real turret, with windows and a window seat. I love it, and so do all my friends.

But although I'm getting used to my new room, getting used to my stepmother and stepsisters hasn't been as easy. For one thing, my stepsisters and I aren't much alike. Jane is nice, but she's majorly into computers. I know how to use the computer at school, but I'm not a disk nerd or anything. And Lucy is a soccer jock. She's on the team at Orlando High. It seems like she's always going to practice or coming from practice. About a week after we moved in together, she asked me if I wanted to work on my back shots with her in the yard. I mean, *back shots*. What the heck are those? Since then, we haven't had much to do with each other.

Now I looked at myself in the mirror. Some princess. I just saw a small, pale third grader with a dorky haircut in a faded, babyish nightgown. Boy, did I really need magic's help! But right now I had to get downstairs. I closed my closet door and yanked open my dresser drawer, just like I do every morning. Then I pulled on a pair of ancient jeans (they were getting a little high-water—I must have grown lately) and a waffle-weave, long-sleeved shirt. I checked myself out in the mirror again. Same old Ella.

I mean, I did have different clothes in the closet. Lame clothes. Clothes that if I wore them, I might as well have a sign saying "I am a dweeb" on my back.

The thing is, my dad is so great. But after my mom died, he had no idea how to dress a girl. So he's always asked my grandmothers and aunts to help. Total disaster! I hate the stuff they pick out.

5

I put on socks and my sneakers and brushed my hair, then ran downstairs. From right outside the kitchen door, I heard Alana say, "Where's Ella?"

"Getting dressed," Lucy said. "How long does it take to put on the same outfit every day?"

I stopped dead. I know Lucy hadn't meant for me to hear that. What a witchy, stepsistery thing to say!

"Lucy!" said Alana. "That is completely uncalled for."

I wanted to storm into the kitchen and tell Lucy that soccer shorts and shin guards weren't exactly a fashion *must*. But then I stopped. Because you know what? Even though Lucy was mean, she was right. I did wear the same dumb thing every day. I probably looked the same as I had in second grade. That was a scary thought.

Ever since I had first realized I was Cinderella, I had always tried to act like the real princess I know I am, no matter what else was going on in my life. But now I realized that acting wasn't enough. I wanted to look like a princess, too.

I was tired of looking like the "before" Cinderella. I wanted to look like the "after"! And I couldn't just hang around, waiting for my fairy godmother to step in and take over. But I also knew I couldn't pull this off by myself.

I had to ask the Disney Girls for help.

Chapter Two

Party!

Eight-forty: The Princess catches the school carriage.

On the school bus, my best friend, Yukiko Hayashi, had saved me a seat.

"Hi!" she said as I slid in next to her. "It's almost chilly today, huh?"

"Yep," I agreed. Even though it was December, it was still about sixty-five degrees outside, and sometimes even warmer. That's one of the great things about living in Orlando. We never have to worry about snow or ice or wearing a million layers of clothes. Once my dad and I went to New York City on vacation. It was colder there in

May than it is here in the middle of winter!

Two blocks away, Ariel Ramos and Paula Pinto got on the bus and sat in front of us. Three blocks after that, Isabelle Beaumont climbed on and sat in back of me and Yukiko. The five of us are all best buds, along with Jasmine Prentiss. (Jasmine doesn't take the school bus, because she lives in Wildwood Estates.) Not only are we all best friends, but we're three pairs of *best* best friends: me and Yukiko, Ariel and Paula, and Isabelle and Jasmine. We're all Disney Girls *and* princesses. But I'll explain about that in a minute.

"Whew! Am I glad it's Friday!" said Ariel, flipping her long red hair over her shoulder. "Weekend, here I come!" She slumped back against the bus seat.

We all laughed. Ariel likes school okay, but she *loves* the weekends.

Soon the bus pulled up to Orlando Elementary and we piled out. Jasmine was waiting for us. The six of us hung out until the bell rang. Then Yukiko, Ariel, and I headed for Ms. Timmons's third-grade class, and Paula, Isabelle, and Jasmine went to Mr. Murchison's fourth-grade class, right across the hall.

I like Ms. Timmons. She's nice, and she doesn't give

tons of homework. She also doesn't let the boys make pains of themselves.

This morning, after she took roll, Ms. Timmons stood at the front of the classroom.

"I have an announcement to make," she said. "Two weeks from today, on the last day of school before winter break, we're going to have a class holiday party."

Yukiko, Ariel, and I made excited faces at each other. I *looove* class parties!

"Take a few minutes to think about what you would like to bring," Ms. Timmons continued. "We'll need refreshments, decorations, music—anything that will make a party fun. I'll pass around a sign-up sheet."

Yukiko and I sit right next to each other. Ariel sits two rows over and one row up. She turned around and gave us a thumbs-up sign. I grinned at her. My mind was already at work, wondering what I should sign up for. I've made sugar cookies a hundred times—and I could decorate them to look holidayish.

"What should I bring?" Yukiko asked, tapping her chin with her finger. "Maybe punch? Or chips and dip? You usually bring sugar cookies, right? They're always yum-ee."

"Yes, I—" I began eagerly, then stopped. There I go

again, I thought. Same old Ella. Same lame clothes, same boring sugar cookies! No wonder I looked like the "before" picture! I *was* the "before" picture! I was even bringing the "before" cookies!

Help me, magic, I pleaded silently. Give me an idea. As soon as I made that wish, a fabulous picture popped into my mind.

"I'm going to bring a gingerbread *castle*," I said, surprising myself. The sign-up paper landed on my desk.

"A gingerbread castle?" Yukiko asked. "Wow. That sounds really hard. Are you sure?"

"Sure I'm sure," I said, trying to sound it. I wrote my name, Ella O'Connor, and next to it wrote: *one gingerbread castle*.

I handed the sheet to Yukiko, who looked impressed. Then I sat back in my desk and straightened all my textbooks so they lined up neatly. I put two sharpened number-two pencils in the pencil slot. Opened my notebook to a fresh sheet.

I was completely ready to start a new day as a new Ella. Look out, world!

Chapter Three

My Best Friend Is a Princess

Twelve o'clock: The Princess dines.

After signing up for the gingerbread castle, I was on a roll. The next major, earth-shattering change I made was trading my bag lunch with Ariel. She gave me her lunch money, and I bought the hot school lunch.

"Fab!" Ariel exclaimed, opening my bag. "A thermos of soup, a ham and cheese sandwich, and a bag of Fritos. Hey, let's do this every day!"

I smiled. My hot lunch was macaroni and cheese, some overcooked broccoli, and a square of spice cake. I dug in, already feeling kind of daring and different.

The six of us Disney Girls always eat lunch together.

Plus, at our school they sometimes put different grades together for classes like art, music, and gym. So we get to see each other every day. It's great.

"The school lunch?" Yukiko looked at me in surprise. "What's up?" She unwrapped her own peanut butter and jelly sandwich.

"I just feel like doing things differently," I explained.

Five pairs of eyes locked on me.

"*You?* Do things differently?" Jasmine said.

"Sure," I said, trying to sound casual. "What's so amazing about that?"

"It's not *amazing*," said Yukiko. "But it is *unusual*. I mean, you're one of the most . . . "

I knew what she was getting at. "Predictable?" I asked. "Boring? Mousy? A big yawn?" I felt myself getting getting steamed. Not at Yukiko—at myself. Why had I waited so long to change?

"I was going to say dependable," said Yukiko.

"Dependable! Ha!" said Ariel. "Dependable is putting it mildly. This is the girl who always wears blue socks on Tuesday."

"I do not!" I said, but I started to smile.

"It's nice that a friend always knows what to expect from you," said Paula, shooting Ariel a glance. "We know we can trust you."

"Oh, come on," I said, leaning my head on my hand. "We can all trust each other. That isn't what I mean."

"Well, what are you going to change?" asked Paula, munching on an apple slice.

"I'm not sure, exactly," I said slowly. "I just know I'm sick of being the 'before' Cinderella." Of course my friends knew what I was talking about. They've known about my being Cinderella for a long time.

I better explain how I found out. When I was really little, my dad took me to see the movie *Cinderella.* It was amazing. It was as if I was watching myself up on the movie screen, except back then I didn't have a stepmother or stepsisters. It wasn't that I *felt* like Cinderella and she felt like me. I just *was* Cinderella. We were the same person.

Anyway, I didn't tell anyone about it, not even my best friend. I had met Yukiko in preschool. We had so much in common—we both loved cats, and chocolate-covered pretzels, and watermelon-flavored lip gloss. Before long we were always hanging out together. We loved to play dress-up and pretend. We had a great time.

In kindergarten, we met Ariel. Ariel is pretty different from me and Yukiko. The two of us are both kind of shy and quiet around people we don't know. Ariel is *never* shy or quiet. Yukiko and I both like to hang out and talk and listen to music and play. Ariel likes to run and jump and

13

climb and swim. But for some reason, Ariel just *fit* with us. The three of us did everything together.

Then Ariel introduced us to *her* best friend, Paula. They live around the corner from each other. Paula and Ariel are both real athletic. We became a foursome.

One day, the four of us were at Paula's house. (My house is really tidy and neat. Paula's house is cluttered and full of animals and books and stuff. It makes me crazy.) It was rainy, and Paula had rented *Pocahontas*. The more I watched the movie, the weirder I felt. Pocahontas was so much like Paula. They looked alike, they sounded alike, they moved the same way. I was wondering whether I should say something. Then Yukiko said in an awed voice, "Paula, it's you. You're Pocahontas."

It all came out after that. Paula felt that she *was* Pocahontas, the exact same way I feel about Cinderella. Then Yukiko confessed she had always known she was Snow White! My own best friend, and I hadn't realized it till then! And guess what else? Ariel is Ariel, the Little Mermaid! *All four of us* were special. We were princesses; we were all touched by magic. It was like waking up and realizing that we were still living a wonderful dream.

Since then, the magic has gotten stronger, and we've

gotten even closer to our princess selves. Two years ago, Jasmine became a Disney Girl, after Yukiko met her in ballet class. She's Princess Jasmine, from *Aladdin*. (She'd thought she was the only one, until she met us!) And this year, Isabelle transferred to Orlando Elementary. She became Jasmine's *best* best friend, even before we figured out that she's Belle, from *Beauty and the Beast*.

Now the six of us are the Disney Girls. We can always depend on each other. And right now, I really needed their help.

Yukiko looked alarmed. "You don't want to change your personality, do you? I like you the way you are."

I giggled. "No! I mean, I wish I weren't so shy in front of strangers, but I don't think I can really change how I am. But maybe I can change how I—*look*, or something. I don't know. I hate my clothes. My hair looks lame. I want to stop doing the same old things all the time. Like signing up for sugar cookies."

"How are you going to change your looks?" Paula asked.

I threw up my hands. "That's just it! I don't know. I don't have a clue about this kind of thing. The whole idea of choosing new clothes just freaks me out. There are too many choices. I don't know what's hot and what's not."

Across the table, Ariel nodded. "You're fashion-

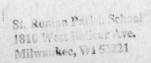

15

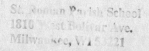

challenged," she said knowingly. "We can help you."

Paula snickered. "Not all of us can get worked up over platform sneakers," she said.

"Hey! They are *adorable*," Ariel said, indignant.

"I have to say," said Isabelle, "that I like clothes, too. I love trying different outfits." Isabelle is African-American, and really pretty. She always looks *together*, like she's wearing her clothes *on purpose*. I never look like that.

Ariel narrowed her eyes and examined me critically. "Okay. Maybe you do need to jazz up your look a little. We'll all help. Anyone up for the mall tomorrow?"

"Yeah, I can make it," said Yukiko. "I'd love to escape from the Dwarfs for a while." Yukiko has *six* little brothers and one baby sister. Since she's Snow White, that makes them the Dwarfs. And did you know that the name Yukiko means "snow child" in Japanese? Cool, huh?

"Count me in," said Paula. She grinned. "I hate shopping, but I have to see this."

"Cool," I said, smiling back.

The six of us agreed to meet at the Clearview Mall the next day. I felt better, knowing that my friends would be there to give me advice and help me pick out some new clothes. Now all I had to do was ask my dad. Oh, and Alana.

Chapter Four

A New Me

Seven-thirty P. M.: The Princess does her homework.

Yep, I get my homework out of the way on Friday night, so I don't have to think about it all weekend. My friends say I'm the most organized person they know—maybe even *too* organized! (Is that possible?) I think it's because for years it was just me and Dad. He's the best dad in the whole world, but he's not really a mom. So I had to learn to handle a lot of things by myself. The older I got, the more things I started organizing, like our grocery shopping, and planning what we would eat all week. It was a lot of work, but I liked being in charge.

Now Alana has pretty much taken over. At first, I didn't like her doing all the things I was used to doing. Especially since she does a lot of things differently than I do. Like, my dad and I used to clean our little apartment ourselves, every Saturday morning. Then we could relax all weekend. Alana hired a housekeeping service to come once a week. To me, it feels weird to have a stranger clean my room.

Another thing is groceries. Dad and I like fun stuff for breakfast, like Toaster Tarts and Pow! cereal with extra Flavor Buds. Since Dad married Alana, I'm lucky to get muesli cereal or shredded wheat, or whole-wheat toast and turkey bacon.

One thing I still organize is *myself*. I keep a schedule so I can stay on top of everything. (Sometimes the Disney Girls tease me about it. But it works for me.) My two stepsisters are pretty disorganized. I can't count how many times they've been late for things, or forgotten their homework, or lost a shoe, or run out of lunch stuff because they didn't put it on the shopping list. Once I showed them my schedule, and offered to help them make their own. They looked at me as if I was from the planet Weird.

So now I was doing my homework on Friday night. *Eight-thirty to nine o'clock: The Princess takes her leisure.*

After I was done, I decided to ask Dad about going shopping. I didn't know how to bring it up. I mean, after my mom died, he had done the best he could about my clothes. I didn't want him to feel bad about it. On the other hand, if I had to wear the same old jeans and shirt combo for the rest of third grade, I would be totally bummed. I went down to the family room, where Dad and Alana were reading. I didn't like talking to him in front of her, but I guessed it was time to get used to it.

"Um, Dad?" I began. He looked up and smiled. "I've been thinking. Maybe I could buy some new clothes."

"New clothes?" He glanced down at my jeans and shirt as if seeing them for the first time. "Hmm," he said.

"That's a great idea!" said Alana, giving Dad a glance.

Gee, Alana agreed easily, I thought. Maybe she had been dying for a chance to fix me up. Was she embarrassed about her new stepdaughter? I mean, obviously Lucy thought I was geeky.

"We could go shopping this weekend, if you like," continued Alana eagerly. "I'm used to shopping for girls." She smiled at me.

"Thanks," I said, trying to remember to be thoughtful and princesslike. "But if it's okay with you, I'd like to go with my friends. They can help me pick out some things."

"Are you sure?" Alana pressed. "I'd be happy to help you."

"Well, maybe this first time I'll go with my friends. Then, if I still need stuff, we can go," I told her.

She didn't look convinced, but Dad got an envelope and put some money into it.

"Thanks, Dad!" I said. "I'll be careful with it."

"Okay. Don't spend it all in one place," he said, ruffling my hair.

"I won't," I promised. I was so excited! Tomorrow was the last day I would be the same old boring *me*!

Saturday, ten o'clock: Princess meets fellow princesses at mall.

The next morning, Dad dropped me off at the mall a few minutes early.

"Thanks, Dad," I said, hopping out of his car. "I'll call you when we're done."

Inside the mall, I picked up a mall map, then sat down on a bench by the fountain. Of course, I'd been here a million times before, so I knew where everything was. But I wanted to work out the best shopping route, so that we would hit all the good stores without backtracking or overlooking anything. I was still hunched over the map, marking a path with my highlighter pen, when my friends started arriving.

"Hey!" called Ariel, running up with Paula. "Ready to get radical?" Ariel's long red hair was braided into four braids. She was wearing a ribbed blue turtleneck sweater that had a huge monkey face embroidered on it. Below that she wore black stove-pipe jeans. Purple high-top sneakers completed her outfit. She looked pretty radical, all right.

"Uh," I stalled. I wanted a new look, but I didn't want anything *too* wild, did I?

Paula answered my silent question. "I don't think radical is really Ella's style," she said. She looked me up and down. "She needs simple, practical clothes. New T-shirts, new jeans. That kind of thing." Paula was wearing a long-sleeved dark blue T-shirt with a picture of two whales swimming on it. Her jeans were just regular, and she wore Birkenstocks with thick socks.

Yukiko came up and smiled at me. "Hi! I've been thinking. Let's go to the Laura Ashley store first. They're having a sale. Their stuff is always so cute." Yukiko herself was wearing a blue and green kilt with a gold pin, and a yellow sweater with a lace collar and little pearl buttons down the back. She always dresses in really girly clothes.

Isabelle and Jasmine arrived together. I waited for them to tell me where to start shopping.

"Hi!" Isabelle said. "I just passed Kokomo's, and they're having a sale. They have some great stuff in there—batik, native prints, kente cloth shawls . . . "

"Or we could go to Sassy Petites," suggested Jasmine. "That's where I get my drawstring pants and crop tops."

I held up my map. "Let's start with Nature Girl," I said. "It's at the north end of the mall. We'll work our way down the east side, then cross over to the west at Jordan's. At twelve o'clock we should be directly across from the food court."

My five friends looked at my map and laughed. Ariel rolled her eyes. "I don't believe this!" she exclaimed, still giggling. "Are you *trying* to suck the fun out of it, or what?"

"I just don't want to waste time," I explained lamely. Maybe sometimes I *did* get a little too organized.

Yukiko put her arm around my shoulders. "It's nice to know that some things will never change," she said.

Paula punched my arm lightly. "Let's go to Nature Girl. That's first on your map, right?"

Chapter Five

The Transformation Continues

Monday, seven forty-three: The Princess gets dressed.

On Monday morning I put on the outfit I had set out the night before. It was the one Paula had loved at Nature Girl. The white microfiber turtleneck had ROCK CLIMBERS ROCK printed on it. The pants were olive-green canvas, with snap-tight ankles and tons of cargo pockets. On top of everything I wore a maroon fleece vest that was rated to twenty degrees below zero. It had been made from recycled plastic soda bottles.

Dressed, I examined myself in the mirror. The clothes were new, and they fit. It definitely looked as if I had gotten dressed *on purpose* this morning. Three big pluses. Did I seem like the "after" Cinderella? I wasn't sure. I didn't look like the same old mousy me, at least.

There was a tap on my door. Lucy stuck her head in my room. "Are you coming—" she began, then she saw me. "Whoa. Climbing Mount Everest today after school?"

"Very funny," I said. "I'm coming in just a second."

Grinning, Lucy shut the door and pounded downstairs. I stuck my nose in the air and followed her.

Everyone looked up when I came into the kitchen. Alana looked a little surprised. Jane grinned. Obviously Lucy had told her about my outfit. I sat down, already feeling too warm inside the fleece vest.

"You look very pretty today, honey," said Dad.

"Thanks," I said. I poured myself some juice.

"Heck, you look downright Olympian," said Lucy, trying not to smile.

I looked at her, trying hard to remember that I was a princess and had to be cool even to my cruel stepsisters. I saw Alana shoot her a warning glance. I poured myself a bowl of muesli.

"Super," Ariel said without enthusiasm. "You're all set to rappel down a cliff."

24

I pulled my hot lunch tray closer. Today we were having Texas Tommies, which are hot dogs filled with cheese and wrapped with bacon. I could practically feel my arteries clogging with fat just looking at it. I picked one up and took a bite.

"You look great," said Paula, sounding pleased. "Those clothes are simple and comfortable, and they'll last forever. Not only that, but Nature Girl gives one percent of their profits to different wildlife preservation groups."

"Oh, yeah, like that's important when it comes to fashion." Ariel rolled her eyes.

Yukiko looked at my clothes doubtfully. "They're kind of . . . tomboyish," she said.

"Nuh-uh," said Paula, frowning. "They're totally perfect for a modern, active woman."

"At least you've got a lot of pockets to put stuff in," said Isabelle. She pointed to one cargo pocket on my leg. "That one's the right size for a little packet of tissues."

"Yeah, and that loop for a rock hammer is going to come in so handy," Ariel said sarcastically. "Here in Florida, where you can't find an actual rock in the entire state."

(Florida is mostly clay, dirt, and swamp. There aren't any mountains or rocky cliffs or anything.)

25

"She might not be in Florida forever!" Paula said defensively.

I sat back and ate my lunch. Usually Paula is the peace-maker—the one who sees both sides to every problem. Usually she and Ariel don't really argue. My friends were getting more worked up about my clothes than I was. I took a sip of milk and sighed to myself. Becoming the "after" Cinderella might be tougher than I thought.

Now that I had gotten my new clothes, it was time to focus on my other big project: the gingerbread castle. On Monday night I made a list. (I love lists. I make them for practically everything!)

castle:

1) recipe
2) pattern
3) ingredients
4) decorations

I looked at my list and nodded. I was ready to tackle the castle.

Chapter Six

Cinderella's Castle

On Tuesday I wore the dress that Yukiko had oohed and aahed over at Laura Ashley. I had to admit, it *was* pretty. It was a lavender floral, with puffy sleeves and a sash tied in the back. I looked pretty dressed up. Was it me? I wasn't sure I wanted to look this girly.

I was just setting my juice on the kitchen table when Lucy pounded downstairs. Jane was right behind her, and Dad came in, holding the morning paper. Alana was feeding her two Siamese cats, Queen and Vlad. (I call them Mean and Bad, because they always try to get to Jaq and Gus.)

"Morning," I said, sitting down and reaching for the toast.

Lucy did an exaggerated double take. "Who are *you*? 'Mary Had a Little Lamb'?"

I took a bite of whole wheat toast.

"You look very pretty, honey," said Dad, kissing the top of my head. "Very grown-up."

I sighed. When would I just look like *me*?

At school Yukiko was thrilled to see what I was wearing. "You look terrific," she said. "You could go anywhere in that dress."

"Yeah, if you have to go have tea with the queen, you're all set," Ariel said. "That dress is so frou-frou!"

"Frou-frou!" said Yukiko. "It is not! It's just pretty."

"Pretty *fancy*," Paula said. "Can you run in it? Can you jump? If you climbed to the top of the monkey bars, everyone would be able to see your underwear."

"It makes your eyes look almost lavender," said Jasmine.

"It *is* a pretty color," said Isabelle. I could tell that was the only nice thing she could think of to say about it.

Well, I was a little tired of thinking about my clothes. The whole clothes thing was giving me a headache.

28

Besides, right now I had to focus on the gingerbread castle situation.

After lunch, Ms. Timmons's class had our weekly library period. I looked up "Gingerbread" on the computer, and got a list of books. Then I found the books and flipped through them to see if they would be useful. Out of five books, one had a good recipe, and one had a couple of pictures of gingerbread houses. I checked them out.

Three-fifteen: The Princess returns to the palace.

After school, I decided I couldn't take the dress anymore. This kind of thing looks great on Yukiko, but Lucy was right: I did sort of look like "Mary Had a Little Lamb." I changed into some jeans and a cotton sweater. The jeans were too short, and were frayed on the bottom. I had spilled bleach on the sweater, so it had white spots on it. I looked like myself again, unfortunately, but at least I was comfortable.

In the kitchen, I pulled out a couple of cookbooks. I compared the gingerbread recipes. None of them said they would make a good gingerbread house. They didn't say they *wouldn't* make good gingerbread houses, either. I decided I would just have to experiment.

I was looking for the baking soda when Alana and Jane got home from a computer club meeting. (Lucy was already home, practicing soccer moves in the backyard.)

"Hi, Ella," said Alana. "What are you up to?"

"I'm making a gingerbread castle for our holiday party at school," I explained. "Right now I'm trying to find the best recipe. Can you tell which one I should use?"

Alana shook her head regretfully. "I'm sorry, but I'm not much of a baker. Could you just buy a gingerbread house?"

"No," I said. "I really want to make one myself."

"It seems awfully complicated," said Alana, looking at a picture of a house in my library book.

"I'll be okay," I said. "Maybe Dad can help me."

Dad didn't know much about gingerbread houses either. So I chose three gingerbread recipes to try. I would use the best one for the gingerbread castle.

After dinner that night, Dad helped me find all the ingredients I needed, and he turned the oven on to pre-heat. Then I got started with recipe #1. I followed the directions exactly, poured the batter into a jelly-roll pan, and put it in the oven.

I set the timer. I knew the gingerbread had to bake into a firm, flat, cookielike thing in order for me to cut it into walls and roofs and doors.

"Umm, that smells good," said Jane, coming into the kitchen.

"Yeah, it does," I said. "I hope it turns out okay."

"Then what?" Jane asked.

"Then I make a note of the exact recipe to use, and I start looking for the perfect pattern," I explained. Jane nodded.

"That's what we do with computers, too," she said. "We break a task down into a bunch of little steps, and do them one at a time. You can solve anything if you do it that way."

I hadn't realized that. To me, computers were a tool to use sometimes to look things up. They didn't interest me more than that. But I could see how Jane would get into them.

Finally the kitchen timer went off. I put on the oven mitts and opened the oven door. I slid out the pan.

"Uh-oh," said Jane, peering over my shoulder.

I stared at the pan in dismay. The gingerbread *smelled* great, but *looked* awful. It wasn't a flat, hard, pan-size cookie. It had tried to become light and cakelike. But the pan was too low, so it had spilled over and risen and toppled and become one huge *mess*!

"Guess that wasn't the recipe," said Jane. "Time to move on to step two."

"Yeah," I said, setting the pan on top of the stove. I broke off a warm piece of gingerbread and ate it. It tasted delicious. But the texture was all wrong. I took out my castle project list and made notes about the recipe: "Too puffy. Not firm. Too cakelike."

Jane and I sat and ate warm, broken gingerbread. Tomorrow I would try again.

Chapter Seven

Castle Panic

Eight-thirty: The Princess catches the school carriage.

"Way to go," said Isabelle when she saw me on the school bus on Wednesday morning. We slapped high fives, but my heart wasn't in it. "You look *totally* glossy."

"Thanks," I said without enthusiasm. Maybe I *looked* glossy, but I didn't *feel* glossy. Today I was wearing flare-leg jeans with an embroidered peasant top. I had a new kente-cloth purse, and I'd pulled my hair back with a headband from Guatemala. I also wore a cowrie-shell necklace.

Isabelle loves ethnic, handcrafted clothes, and she looks

great in them. But I felt as if I had a neon sign flashing over my head. My outfit was interesting, sure, but I didn't want to stand out *that* much. Was there any outfit anywhere that would make me feel as good as I looked?

"How did your gingerbread come out last night?" Yukiko asked as I sat down next to her.

I groaned. "It was a disaster. I'm going to try recipe number two tonight."

"Have you found a good pattern for the castle yet?" asked Paula.

"No," I said, shaking my head. "There don't seem to be any patterns for a castle at all. I'm probably going to combine a couple of the house patterns that I've found."

"Jeez, this is getting to be a real pain," said Ariel. "Maybe it's not too late to change your mind."

"I don't want to change my mind," I said. "I'm sure I can do it. It's just a matter of getting all the details right."

"Well, let us know if we can help," said Yukiko. "And I like your headband."

That night I mixed up gingerbread batch #2. Alana was doing some paperwork in the kitchen as I worked.

"I'm so impressed that you chose to tackle something so

difficult," she said. "I've never been very comfortable in the kitchen. My mother is a great cook, but she never let us kids in there while she was cooking, so none of us inherited her skills."

"Oh," I said, looking at Alana. This was interesting. I like it when adults tell me real stories about their lives. Sometimes grown-ups make it sound like everything was always wonderful when they were little. And I sit there and think, *I'm so sure.*

I stirred in some powdered ginger and cinnamon. This dough was very stiff, and my arm was getting tired. Finally it was ready. Last night I had just poured the batter into the pan, but this batter was much drier. I dumped it out and flattened it down with a rolling pin dusted with flour. It was like leather.

I put it on a cookie sheet and popped it in the oven.

Next I turned my attention to my house patterns. Basically, I needed four wall pieces and two roof pieces for a simple house. But I wanted to do a real castle, with turrets and a drawbridge. I traced a house pattern from one book. Of course, it was much too small. I tried to draw it larger onto a new sheet. But it was so hard—everything had to be made evenly bigger. It was so frustrating!

Finally I tore up my pattern and started over.

"Are you having trouble?" asked Alana.

"Trouble with what?" Jane said, coming into the kitchen. Lucy was right behind her, carrying an empty glass.

Just then the timer went off, and I grabbed the oven mitts. I pulled the cookie sheet out of the oven.

"Smells great," said Jane. "Yum."

I looked at the gingerbread happily. It looked as if this had been the right recipe. The dough had hardly risen at all. It was baked to a nice, flat, even brown. It smelled sweet and spicy. My mouth watered. "We have to let it cool for a minute, then we can taste it," I said.

"Okay," said Jane. "Now, what are you having trouble with?"

"The dumb pattern," I said. "It's making me crazy. But I'll figure it out," I added quickly.

Jane looked over my drawings, and at the pattern in the book. "I could scan this in on the computer, and make it bigger," she said. "You could even change the design."

Sure, I thought. Just because I'm younger than her didn't mean I couldn't do anything on my own! After all, I had been doing things myself for practically my whole life. Now that I had a stepmother and two stepsisters, I hadn't suddenly become helpless or anything.

"Thanks, but I guess I better do it myself," I said.

Jane shrugged. "Whatever."

"At least use graph paper to make the pattern bigger," said Lucy. "Look, draw a regular one on graph paper. Then copy it onto another sheet. But for every one square on the little pattern, use four squares on the new page. Then your pattern will be much bigger."

Although I didn't want help, Lucy's idea made a lot of sense. "Wow," I said. "That's a good idea. I didn't even think about graph paper."

"We use it in algebra," Lucy said. "I have some. I'll go get it."

Alana smiled at me, and I could tell she was glad that the three of us were getting to be more like real sisters.

I got a butter knife and began to cut the gingerbread. Or at least, I tried to cut it. It wouldn't cut.

"Here," said Lucy, coming back with a packet of paper.

"Thanks," I grunted, trying to force the knife into the huge cookie.

"Be careful," warned Alana. "Let me try."

I handed her the knife and she tried to slice the

37

gingerbread. She pushed hard, but nothing happened. She looked at me in surprise. Then she really leaned on the knife and pounded the handle with our meat mallet. At last the gingerbread cracked apart, like a piece of slate.

"Whoa," said Jane. "Some gingerbread."

I picked up a chunk and tried to bite it. It was rock-hard. I could barely gnaw off a small bite. Jane tried to bite it too, but stopped and put it down.

"This stuff will wreck my braces," she said.

Dropping my piece, I wailed, "I can't make a house out of this!"

"Maybe you could make, like, a gingerbread *prison*," said Lucy.

"What went wrong?" asked Alana.

"I don't know," I said. "I guess it's back to the beginning. Again."

Chapter Eight

Disney Girls to the Rescue!

At the mall last weekend, I had been so happy and excited to be buying all my new different outfits. Each one had seemed adorable and perfect. Now every morning I looked at them and wondered if my brain had been on vacation.

On Thursday I wore what Jasmine had raved over at Sassy Petites. The hip-hugger corduroy pants weren't too bad, but when I paired them with a crop-top sweater, I looked as if I had shrunk everything in the wash. For some reason, Jasmine can wear this kind of stuff all the time. But on me it just looked dumb. I frowned at myself in the mirror. I tugged the sweater down to cover my stomach. So far in the fashion department I was up to four strikes, no runs.

On the school bus that morning, Ariel looked me up and down. "Not bad," she said.

"I can see your belly button," Yukiko said.

I tugged my sweater lower.

Paula leaned over our bench seat. "You're going to catch cold with your stomach hanging out like that."

I tugged my sweater down harder, and tried to hitch the pants up. My stomach wasn't exactly "hanging out," but you could see my belly button every time I raised my arms. I leaned my head against the window. Was it too late to pretend to be sick today?

Just as we pulled up to school, Jasmine jumped out of her mother's car. She waited for us as we got off the bus.

"Now, *that's* an outfit," she told me with a big smile. "You look great. Like you're already in fourth grade."

Since I usually look as if I'm in *second* grade, not third, I guessed I was making progress. But it didn't feel like it.

Two o'clock: The Princess has gym.

At Orlando Elementary, they put the third- and fourth-grade classes together for gym. (They usually separate the girls from the boys, thank goodness.) I really like it, because it gives you a big mix of people for teams. Today I was also relieved to get out of my new clothes and put on my gym stuff.

First we started class with twenty minutes of aerobics to music. Then Ms. Lu, the girls' gym teacher, told us to do two laps around the entire schoolyard. Ariel and Paula immediately took off, trying to beat each other and everyone else. They love stuff like this. Yukiko, Jasmine, Isabelle, and I kept up a steady pace that still allowed us to talk.

"I've decided to make almond cookies for our party next Friday," Yukiko said, panting a little. "Mom said she would help me."

"I love your almond cookies," I said, pumping my arms.

"Isabelle and I are signed up for decorations for our class party," Jasmine as she pounded next to us. "I'm not sure what we'll do yet."

My friends waited for me to give a progress report on my gingerbread castle. I jogged along.

"Well?" Yukiko finally demanded.

I made a face. "I still haven't gotten too far with it," I admitted. "But I have a whole week left."

Ariel and Paula had lapped us, and were jogging with us again.

"You could just make a sheet cake of gingerbread," suggested Paula. She wasn't even breathing hard. "With cream-cheese icing. That would be great, and you could cut it into squares."

"I guess I could," I grumbled. "But that's something the 'before' Cinderella would do. I have my heart set on doing something fabulous. Something princessy." Secretly, I wished I had signed up for decorations. Then I could just twist some crepe paper together and call it a day.

"Well, it sounds like you need help," Paula said. She doesn't beat around the bush. "Look, my dad's an engineer. He designs things all the time. Can I ask him to design a simple castle? One that could be baked? He could make the pattern and everything."

As this idea began to sink into my mind, my heart suddenly felt a little lighter. Before I could answer, Isabelle said, "My mom knows a lot about food and recipes." (Mrs. Beaumont owns Beaumont's, which is a fancy gourmet-food shop.) "If it's okay with you, I'll ask her if she knows the right gingerbread recipe to use for a house."

"I could borrow my mom's cake-decorating kit," said Yukiko. "It has all different tips and nozzles. You could make the icing look like icicles or swirls or flowers or anything."

The six of us trotted up to the gym doors, where Ms. Lu was waiting with her clipboard. "Good time, girls," she said. "We're going to play a quick game of basketball, so head on inside."

"How about it?" asked Paula, once we were inside. "Should I ask my dad?"

I made a lightning-fast decision. "Yes!" I said. "That would be great. If I don't get this together, I'll end up at the holiday party with a store-bought bag of ginger-snaps."

My friends laughed. A huge weight had been lifted off my shoulders. So far, my gingerbread castle had been a big failure. But now I had the Disney Girls' help. With them on my side, I knew there was no stopping me.

Chapter Nine

The Last Straw

When Lucy came down to breakfast on Friday, she took one look at me and staggered back.

"Oh my gosh!" she said, covering her eyes. "I think I've gone blind!" She staggered backward and bumped into a cabinet.

My cheeks burned, but what could I say? I probably *had* made her go blind.

Today I was wearing the outfit Ariel had said was the hottest, coolest, glossiest outfit at Zap 2000, her favorite store at Clearview Mall. It was a zebra-striped, long-sleeved swing top made out of sweatshirt material, with

44

bright red patch pockets. Under it I wore black and white Dalmatian-spotted leggings. On my feet were—you guessed it—platform sneakers. Red ones. They squeaked on the kitchen floor. They made me almost three inches taller. My hair was held back by a black headband with red pom-poms.

I sat down at my place and poured myself a bowl of cereal.

"Golly," said Dad, coming in with the newspaper. "Is that one of your new outfits?"

"Yep," I said.

"It's very . . . mod," Dad said uncertainly. "But you look very pretty, honey."

Jane and Lucy looked at him in disbelief.

I sighed to myself. Poor Dad. "Thanks," I said.

Jane sat across from me and poured milk onto her cereal. "Well, it looks . . . comfortable," she said.

"Yep," I said. I didn't want to talk about it.

"Oh, so cool!" Ariel cried when she saw me. "You look— totally awesome. That's all I can say."

I plunked down in my school bus seat next to Yukiko. She looked at me and smiled, but didn't mention my clothes. Neither did Paula or Isabelle. I didn't blame them.

45

At school, Jasmine nodded and smiled when she saw me. "I had forgotten about Ariel's outfit," she said.

"How could you forget *this*?" I asked, gesturing at myself.

"It *is* pretty . . . unforgettable," Yukiko said.

"*Totally* unforgettable!" said Ariel happily.

"Holy moley!" cried Jason Heidenberger, when I walked into Ms. Timmons's class. "What's black and white and red all over?"

I glared at him and raised my lip in a snarl.

"Don't listen to him," Ariel advised. "He's still wearing Grranimals."

"Am not!" said Jason.

Ariel stuck her tongue out at him and sat down at her desk.

I slid into my own desk, next to Yukiko's. This is it, I thought. This is the last straw. Next week I would wear my same old boring clothes. At least then people wouldn't tease me about it. At least then I wouldn't feel like the poster girl for the society of fashion victims.

I was doomed to be the "before" Cinderella forever.

At lunchtime on Friday, I waited until my friends and I

were seated at our usual table. Then I took a list out of my pocket.

"Okay," I read. "Number one. Castle design from Mr. Pinto?" I raised my eyebrows at Paula.

"Bad news, Ella," Paula said, looking sorry. "My dad's leaving today on a business trip. He won't be back for a week. So he couldn't make you a pattern for the castle. But he did draw you a little castle picture." She pulled a piece of paper out of the pocket of her painter pants. It was a line drawing of a simple castle. I squinted at it, trying to imagine it as a cake.

"He said it would be pretty easy to break it down into parts and make a pattern," said Paula. "Maybe if we all work on it together . . . "

"No, this is great," I said. I smiled at her and checked off item one from my list. "Tell your dad thanks for me. Now, item two . . . Mrs. Beaumont's recipe?"

"Here," said Isabelle, handing me a photocopy. "She says she's used this before. It'll be flat and firm, like a cookie. Easy to cut and build with."

"But not like cement," I said. My friends laughed. I had told them about my batch of indestructible gingerbread.

"Yeah," said Isabelle, opening her stainless-steel

lunch box. "Mom said if you want her to come over and help you—"

"Oh, thanks," I said. "That's really nice of her." I checked off item two and opened my milk carton. Today the hot lunch was a small slab of meat loaf with ketchup, mixed vegetables, and some canned pears. Ugh. I was starting to miss my nice lunches from home. "Now—item three. Mrs. Hayashi's cake-decorating kit. Yukiko?"

"It's in my cubby," Yukiko said. "Remind me to give it to you before we go home."

"Okay," I said. "I can't wait to use it." I checked off item three, pleased. I love it when I have a list with everything checked off.

"It takes practice," Yukiko warned. "But Mom said she'd be happy to show you how."

"Thanks so much, guys," I said. "You've saved me. But I'll try to do it myself, first. I'll yelp for help if I need it."

"Okay," said Yukiko. "After all, you have a whole week."

"Sure," I said. "No problem."

That night, armed with Isabelle's mother's secret recipe, I headed into the kitchen once again. I had already tried twice. Maybe three would be the magic number. I got organized, pulling out bowls, collecting ingredients, preheating the oven. Then I started beating butter and sugar together.

I worked very quickly. Soon I was smoothing the batter onto the baking sheet. I popped it in the oven, set the timer, and sat back to wait.

"One more try, huh?" asked Jane, coming in to get a glass of milk. "Got a pattern yet?"

"Almost," I said. "I think it's under control."

"Good," said Jane. "Yell if you need help."

"Okay, thanks," I said.

The delicious smell of ginger and spices filled the kitchen. Soon my dad drifted in, followed by Alana.

"That smells terrific," Alana said. "This time I think you've got it. I've been thinking—I can't help you with the baking, but I bet I could do some decorating. After all, I *am* a real estate agent. I know how to make a house look its best." She smiled at me.

I smiled back. "Thanks. I'll let you know." It was nice of her, but I really wanted to do the whole thing by myself. When the timer went off, I put on the oven mitts and took out the baking sheet.

"Hmm," Dad said.

I stared at it in horror. Instead of a smooth, brown cookie, I had a puffy, bubbly mess! It was burned almost black around the edges, and was totally uncooked in the middle. What had gone wrong?

"I do not *believe* this!" I exclaimed. "This was Mrs. Beaumont's secret recipe! Tried and true!"

"Maybe she wrote down the wrong thing," Alana suggested.

I shook my head. "She photocopied the actual cookbook."

"Did you do everything correctly?" Dad asked gently.

Seven-forty: The Princess freaks out.

All of a sudden, I had had enough of this stupid gingerbread castle. "No," I said, taking off the oven mitts and flinging them on the counter. "I made a huge mistake—thinking I could even do this!" I thought about the clothes I had been wearing all week. I thought about eating yucky school hot lunches. My eyes got hot. I was about to burst into tears.

"Nothing is going right!" I said. "My whole life is a disaster!" Then I dumped the ruined gingerbread into the sink and ran to my room.

Chapter Ten

Princesses Just Want to Have Fun

I was still crying on my bed when Dad came into my room.

For a few minutes he sat next to me, stroking my hair and patting my back. After a while I started hiccuping.

"Nothing is going right," I finally said. Dad handed me a tissue and I wiped my eyes and nose.

"Like what?" asked Dad. "Let's make a list."

I couldn't help smiling a little bit. He knows that I make lists for everything. "Well, like my stupid, horrible gingerbread disaster," I said. "That's number one."

"Okay," said Dad, holding up one finger. "What else?"

"My stupid, horrible clothes," I said. "All week I haven't felt like myself. I don't know what to do."

"Okay, that's two," said Dad. Two fingers.

"My lunches," I mumbled. "I'm sick of the cafeteria lunches. I want to bring my lunch from home again."

"That's an easy one to fix," said Dad, grinning. "I don't think we need to put it on the list. You know what? We can't solve your clothes or your gingerbread problem right now, tonight. But you need to take a break from worrying about all this stuff. You've been trying to make gingerbread all week. You've been worried about clothes all week. Take the weekend off, don't think about your problems, and have a good time with your friends. On Monday, we'll tackle everything that's going wrong."

"That sounds good," I said, sniffling.

"You just need something to perk you up," said Dad.

"Maybe so," I said. I felt much better.

On Saturday morning, I put on my regular clothes. I checked myself out in the mirror. I still felt unhappy with how I looked. I had tried changing my style, but it hadn't helped much. What else could I do?

Hmm. My hair. I never paid much attention to my

hair. Now I saw that it looked kind of scraggly. A haircut! That was something I could do to perk myself up.

I ran downstairs to the kitchen and asked Dad if I could have a haircut.

"Well, sure, I guess," said Dad. He reached for his wallet. "Here's fifteen bucks. You can go to Dimecuts."

"Thanks, Dad!" I said, reaching for the money.

"Oh, no," said Alana, looking up from her cup of tea. "Not Dimecuts! Ella should have a new hairstyle—definitely. But she can go to Henri. That's where the girls and I get our hair done."

"Dimecuts is okay," I said.

"No indeed," said Alana firmly. "In fact, I have an appointment this morning with Henri myself. I'll take you instead. How's that?"

Dad smiled at Alana, pleased. What could I do? Henri would probably do a better job than Dimecuts anyway. I smiled at Alana. "Okay, thanks."

Like I said, I'm kind of shy in new situations. Sometimes the only thing that helps me is to remember that I'm a princess.

Henri's Chic Styles was a really fancy place. It had dark

marble floors, pale pink walls, and fancy art with gold frames. As soon as we walked in, I wanted to walk right out again. I wished I could have gone to Dimecuts. But Alana ushered me in and introduced me to the appointment lady.

Then we sat down on a blue velvet couch. An assistant appeared and brought Alana a cup of tea.

"Thank you, Michelle," said Alana.

Michelle offered me a soda. Would I have to pay for it? I didn't know what to do. "No, thank you," I mumbled.

I swung my feet against the couch for a long time while Alana read magazines. Sometimes people said hello to her and chatted. I felt so dumb and out of place. At least I wasn't wearing my usual clothes. Before we had left the house, Alana had come into my room.

"Maybe you should change," she suggested casually. "So you don't get hair all over your favorite clothes." Then she opened my closet door. First she tossed Paula's cargo pants on the bed, then Jasmine's cropped sweater. I groaned silently at the thought of wearing them again.

But you know what? They looked good together. The cargo pants came up high enough that my stomach didn't show every time I raised my arms. And the sweater looked better with the cargo pants than the turtleneck and vest had.

"Good," said Alana, looking me up and down. She smiled. "I told you I'm used to dressing girls."

I smiled back, but inside I felt confused. On the one hand, Alana definitely knew more about clothes than Dad or I did. On the other hand, I almost felt guilty. If I let Alana start taking over, would it mean that Dad hadn't been a good enough dad?

Finally it was my turn. Another assistant led us back into a small private room. I was glad I wouldn't have my hair cut out in front where everyone could see.

"Henri, this is my stepdaughter, Ella," said Alana. "She's looking for a whole new style. What do you think about one of those modern, layered cuts?"

My eyes widened. I didn't want anything *too* trendy— even though Ariel would love it.

"*Non,*" said Henri, with a French accent. He squinted his dark eyes at me and pursed his lips. I felt like an insect. Remember, you're a princess, I told myself. I held my head a little higher.

"I see somesing simple, *très classique,*" he pronounced. He clapped his hands and a young woman came to shampoo me. As I leaned back in the chair with my head over the basin, I closed my eyes and made a desperate wish:

All the magic powers that be,
Hear me now, my special plea.
I want to be the best, true me—
Please help me see what I could be.

An hour later, I stared at myself in the mirror. I really *was* a princess! Henri had hardly changed anything, but he had changed everything! My hair was practically the same length as before, but now it was swingy and cute. It came down to my chin in front and barely brushed my shoulders in back. Instead of looking scraggly, it looked sensational!

"I love it!" I said happily.

"I like it, too," said Alana, smiling at me. "It looks terrific. Thank you, Henri."

"Yes, thank you, Henri," I said as I climbed down from the chair. "It's great."

Henri looked pleased as he surveyed my hair one last time. "Yes, eet ees perfect," he declared. Then he frowned. "But it does not go wis dat outfit."

On Sunday, the Disney Girls decided to meet at the mall again.

"Oh, cool!" exclaimed Jasmine when she saw me. "Your hair is awesome!"

"Thanks," I said, smiling. "I really like it too."

"It looks fabulous," Yukiko agreed. "Did you go to Dimecuts?"

I shook my head. "Alana took me to her stylist."

"Whoa, fancy-schmancy," said Ariel. "It looks great."

Thank you, Henri, I thought. And thank you, magic, for helping Henri.

"You know, we could catch the one o'clock show of *The Sorcerer's Battle*," said Isabelle, looking at her watch.

Jasmine grinned. "Is that another sword-and-wizard movie?"

"Yeah," Isabelle admitted. She loves wizards and witches and medieval stories.

"Sounds good to me," I said.

We had to walk through the whole shopping center to get to the theater. The mall was decorated for the holidays, with red poinsettias everywhere, and a huge Christmas tree covered with Japanese paper origami decorations. In another wing of the mall, a large wooden menorah was set up with one candle lit, for Hanukkah. There was a special Kwanzaa table covered with a beautiful cloth in front of one of the stores. On it were bowls of corn, fruit, and grains, symbolizing the successful harvest.

It felt super festive and holidayish. As long as I didn't think about my gingerbread castle, I was happy. While we were walking around, we played one of our special Disney Girl games. It's not really a game—it's just something we do.

Jasmine is Princess Jasmine, from *Aladdin*, right? So while we walked around, we pretended that we were all her royal friends, and that we had sneaked out of the Sultan's palace.

For just a moment we linked pinkies and closed our eyes. When I opened my eyes again, instead of Clearview Mall, decorated for Christmas, I was in the marketplace of Agrabah. It was hot and dusty and filled with unusual smells that tickled my nose: spices, fruits, leather . . .

I felt as if I were wearing a long, flowing outfit, with a thin shawl covering my hair. The six of us walked through the marketplace, staring at all the wonderful new things we were seeing. There were piles of sweet dates, small wooden tables and boxes inlaid with gold and mother-of-pearl, beautiful cotton and silk cloth.

It was so, so magical. That's one of the coolest things about being a Disney Girl—the magic that's part of our lives, practically every day. Finally, though, it was lunchtime.

"Let's buy some food from that vendor over there," Princess Jasmine said. "Did anyone bring money, or should we charge it to the sultan?"

We all giggled, and the spell was broken.

"I guess the sultan wouldn't be too crazy about that idea," Jasmine admitted.

The six of us grabbed a table in the food court. We each got a different thing and shared it. I had some pizza, an egg roll, a bite of a hot dog, part of a taco, some steamed vegetables and rice, and some curly fries.

After lunch, it was time for Isabelle's movie. Even though it wasn't really my kind of thing, I still enjoyed it. Isabelle loved it.

That afternoon, when Dad picked me up to go home, I felt like a new person. That's what having great friends (and a little magic!) can do for you.

Chapter Eleven

One Step Forward,
Two Steps Back

As Dad had promised, on Monday we began to tackle my problems. That night after dinner, Dad read me the recipe out loud while I assembled the ingredients and made the dough. This time, I realized what I had done wrong. Instead of putting in three teaspoons of baking soda, I had put in three teaspoons of cornstarch! The boxes looked a lot alike. No wonder it hadn't turned out well.

Guess what? This time, the gingerbread came out *perfectly*! It looked like a huge, flat, rectangular cookie. It smelled great. It tasted great. It was firm enough to cut and build with, but soft enough to eat without breaking your teeth.

I was doing a happy dance around the kitchen when Jane came in.

"Hey, can I try some?" she asked.

"Sure," I said, skipping around, carrying used bowls to the sink.

"Umm, this is good," she said, chewing. "Now all you have to do is build a castle out of it."

I quit skipping. Jane was right. Victory was not mine yet. I was not ready to walk into Ms. Timmons's classroom on Friday and totally impress my classmates. I looked at Dad.

"Tomorrow," he said. "You can do step two tomorrow."

On Tuesday I tried five times to create a usable pattern from the little drawing that Mr. Pinto had done for me. I ended up ripping them into pieces.

On Wednesday I decided to make a simple house instead. Four walls and a two-piece roof that looked like a big triangle. I made two sheets of flat gingerbread, cut them out, and tried to stand them up and stick them together with icing. I couldn't get them to stick together, and finally I fiddled with them so much they broke into a million pieces.

The first thought I had on Thursday morning when I woke up was: I am toast. I am completely ruined. I am *waaaay* past my sell-by date.

I could hardly get out of bed. Somehow I managed to feed Jaq and Gus. They squeaked at me. I had been so busy lately I had hardly had time to play with them. I got dressed in Jasmine's corduroys and a plain white turtleneck sweater that Aunt Barbara had given me. The sweater had come with plaid bows and small gold bells sewn all over it. I know—weird, huh? I cut them all off, and now it looked okay. In fact, the pants and sweater together didn't look half bad. They looked better than I felt, anyway.

At school I slunk into Ms. Timmons's class and put my head down on my arms. I had hardly spoken to my friends on the bus.

"What's the matter, Ella?" asked Yukiko in a concerned whisper. "Are you sick?"

I shook my head.

"Did you have an argument with your stepmother or stepsisters?" asked Ariel.

"No," I mumbled into my elbow. "We hardly ever argue anymore."

"Then tell us what's wrong," Yukiko begged. "Remember, we're your best friends. You can tell us anything."

I raised my head. "It's my gingerbread castle," I whispered. "It's a total meltdown. I need help, and I need it bad. I'll tell you about it at lunch."

Twelve o'clock: The Princess dines.

"Okay, now spill," commanded Yukiko once we were all sitting at our usual lunch table.

I opened the bag I had brought from home. I was glad to be eating normal food again. One problem solved. Big whoop.

Trying not to feel too sorry for myself, I gave my friends the rundown on the list of disasters that had struck this week.

"Now it's Thursday," I pointed out. "The class holiday party is *tomorrow*. And I have *nothing*! Nothing to bring to the party. Nothing to show for two weeks of work." I wanted to go home, climb into bed, and stay there for a month.

"Look," said Paula, "you do have a recipe that works, right?"

"Right," I said.

"That's half the battle," said Yukiko.

"No, it's only one-third the battle," I said grumpily. "I still need the perfect pattern *and* I have to decorate it."

"Are you really sure you don't want to bring a nice sheet cake?" Jasmine asked.

I grimaced. "The whole class knows I signed up for a gingerbread castle. They're *expecting* a gingerbread castle. Or at least a gingerbread house."

"There's only one thing to do," said Ariel. "We all have to come to your house tonight and help you. It's the only way you'll get it done. With the DGs working together, we can conquer this castle."

She sounded so sure that she almost convinced me.

"Really?" I asked. "You think?"

"We'll be there at seven," Isabelle promised.

Chapter Twelve

Help, Disney Girls!

On Thursday evening, as soon as supper was over, I raced around, setting out mixing bowls, cookie sheets, all the candies and decorating stuff, and icing mix. I checked everything off my list. When the doorbell rang, I was ready.

"We're here!" Yukiko called as she came into the kitchen.

"We're gonna whip that house into shape!" Ariel yelled, flinging her coat down on a chair.

"Hi, girls," said Alana, coming into the kitchen. "It's kind of chilly outside, isn't it? Why don't you fix some hot

65

chocolate? Making gingerbread castles can be hard work."

"Thanks, Alana," I said.

"She seems nicer than she used to," Yukiko whispered after Alana had left.

I nodded. "I think we're all getting used to living together." I nuked six mugs of instant hot chocolate in the microwave. Then we rolled up our sleeves and got to work.

Soon Ariel and Yukiko were busily stirring up batches of gingerbread dough. Paula was shaking a big Ziploc baggie full of shredded coconut and a few drops of green food coloring. It already looked like grass. Jasmine was taping chocolate kisses to the twigs of a small branch. It would be a tree in the yard. Isabelle was carefully cutting out a wax-paper pattern of a house wall, with a door and two windows. So it wouldn't be a castle. My classmates would have to live with it. I turned on the oven and starting rolling out the dough so it would be smooth and flat.

By eight o'clock, we had four sheets of beautiful, perfect gingerbread. It was all we could do to keep from devouring it right there. It smelled and looked delicious! I knew with my friends' help (and a little magic), everything would turn out!

Yukiko started mixing vanilla frosting with the electric mixer. Ariel decided to whip up one more batch of dough so we would have extra, just in case. Paula had finished the coconut grass, and was getting ready to melt some hard candies in the microwave to make windows.

"Oops, sorry," Paula said, bumping Ariel's elbow.

"Yow! Watch it!" Ariel said. "Look what you did." She pointed to her shirt, which she had spilled flour on.

Paula giggled. "You look like Casper the Friendly Ghost."

"Oh, you think it's funny, huh?" said Ariel. Quickly she picked up a measuring spoon and flung a spoonful of flour right at Paula's face.

"Oh!" Paula and Ariel both gasped in surprise.

I looked up just as Yukiko whirled around to see what was happening. Unfortunately, she forgot to turn off the mixer. Still spinning fast, the beaters sprayed icing all over everything!

"Oh, no!" cried Yukiko, slamming the mixer back down into the frosting. She turned it off. Before I could even scrape icing off me, Paula blinked slowly, her eyes dark in her white powdery face. Even her hair was coated with flour. I looked at Ariel.

Ariel seemed shocked by what she had done. Her blue eyes big, she stared at Paula. Then, even though she was obviously trying to keep a straight face, she let out a tiny giggle. Then a bigger giggle. She covered her mouth with her hand and tried to smother a laugh. It was no use. Ariel started guffawing loudly, pounding the countertop and pointing at Paula, who really did look like Casper the Friendly Ghost.

As Isabelle, Yukiko, Jasmine, and I stared in fascinated horror, Paula's eyes narrowed, and she smiled an alligator-like smile. It didn't seem like she was truly mad, but she was definitely determined. As Ariel gasped for breath, Paula wheeled around, grabbed the pastry bag full of vanilla icing, pointed it at Ariel, and squeezed hard.

Zzzziiiip! A thin stream of icing shot out the bag and curled up neatly on Ariel's face. Ariel gasped again, this time in surprise, and her mouth forming in a big O.

"Um, guys," I said, "let's just take it easy. We have to finish this."

"Yeah, come on," said Isabelle, opening the package of food coloring. "I have to go home by nine o'clock. Quit messing around." She took out the little bottle of blue food coloring and gave it a hard, professional shake. But she squeezed too hard! The cap flew off, and a splotch of dark-blue food coloring shot up onto her face.

I couldn't believe this was happening.

Isabelle looked so surprised, with the blue dye dripping off her nose.

Suddenly all six of us were laughing hysterically. Isabelle had a big blue splotch on her face, Ariel was coated with icing, Paula was white with flour, and the rest of us had been sprayed with frosting. Could things get any worse?

They could. Laughing hard, I stumbled against one of the trays of gingerbread. I tried to catch it, but it slipped through my fingers and fell to the floor with a big crash. The sheet of gingerbread broke into a thousand pieces.

I quit laughing.

"Oh, I'm so sorry, Ella," said Yukiko, catching her breath.

I gazed in horror at the mess on the floor.

"We have this other batch ready to go," said Ariel.

"Girls, is everything okay?" asked Alana, coming into the kitchen. "What was that noi—" She stopped dead when she caught a glimpse of us, and the kitchen. She looked around at the disaster area; then her eyes focused on me.

"This is not what I had in mind when I said your friends could come over to help you," she said, sounding angry. "I suggest you clean this mess up, and then I think your friends should call their parents to come get them."

I was mortified. My dad had never, ever sent my friends home before. Before I could reply, Alana turned and stalked out of the kitchen, her back stiff.

For a few moments we were all silent, shocked.

"I'm really sorry, Ella," Ariel said softly. "This is all my fault."

"It doesn't matter whose fault it is," I said miserably. "This place is a mess. Now Alana's mad, and I still don't have a castle, a house, or even a gingerbread *hut*!"

Trying not to cry, I wet a sponge and started cleaning icing off the cabinets.

Chapter Thirteen

Complete Castle Meltdown

It didn't take all that long to clean the kitchen. It had looked worse than it was. Paula, Ariel, and Isabelle finally went home to take showers. After giving me a supportive hug, Yukiko and Jasmine left, too.

Alone in the kitchen, I surveyed the situation. I'd had to throw away a whole sheet of gingerbread. I put Ariel's backup sheet into the oven and set the timer. I still had the icing, the decorations, and the flat board to build the house on. It all seemed so overwhelming. It was already nine-thirty, and I was tired and in a bad mood. I still didn't have a good pattern to use. I didn't know what to do first. The whole project seemed impossible, and I didn't know where to begin. For once, I couldn't break things down into little steps. I couldn't make a list. I was humongously sick of the whole thing.

Alana came back into the kitchen just as I took the baked gingerbread out of the oven. I was really angry at her, and embarrassed because she had sent my friends home.

"The kitchen looks much better," Alana said, sounding a little stiff.

I didn't say anything. I pretended to be examining my pattern, and wrinkled my forehead to make it look as if I were considering what to do first.

"I'm sorry I had to send your friends home," said Alana. "But I felt that you all weren't respecting the fact that this is my house, too, and Jane and Lucy's. Things you do affect more than just you and your dad."

I felt my chin get firm, the way it does right before I say something I usually am sorry for later.

"What about how what *you* do affects *me*?" I asked, pointing around the kitchen. "How am I supposed to make this gingerbread castle now? Look at it! It's in pieces. I don't have a pattern, I don't know what to do. I really, really needed my friends' help. And *you* sent them home." I rubbed my eyes, feeling the tears beginning to well up. "I've been working on this thing for two weeks, and don't have anything to show for it. And it's due tomorrow!" I started crying, and felt so mad at myself for crying in front of Alana.

"You know, Ella," said Alana, "we all offered to help you last week. Jane could have made you a good pattern on her computer. You said no, thanks. And while I'm not good at baking, I offered to help with the decoration. But you didn't want our help. You wouldn't even let me help you go shopping—and now you're unhappy with all your new clothes."

I cried quietly, but I was listening. It was true—but I had liked the outfit she put together, and I loved my new haircut that she had helped with.

"We're a family now, Ella," Alana continued, more gently. "Families help each other and support each other. We wanted to be that for you, but you wouldn't let us. We're not here to just—get in your way."

With a sense of surprise, I realized that was sort of how I saw them. Had I been wrong? I felt so wiped out. I couldn't stop crying. If I didn't show up tomorrow with at

73

least a gingerbread house, I would never be able to hold my head up at school again.

"Look," said Alana, coming over and handing me a tissue. "You're worn out. Why don't you go calm down in your room for a little while? Wash your face, change your clothes, and rest for ten minutes. Then come back out and we can decide what you need to do. Okay?"

I nodded and stumbled my way upstairs. In the bathroom I splashed cold water on my face until I stopped crying. I got most of the icing out of my cute haircut. In my room, I peeled off my sticky, floury clothes and put on some comfy sweats. Then I lay down on my bed and closed my eyes.

Maybe Alana had been right. Maybe I should have let them help me. The thing was, I was used to my friends helping me. I knew I would help them back when they needed it. I wasn't used to having a whole new family who would help, too. And I didn't know how I would feel if they needed *my* help. I think I was just trying to keep them out of my life as much as possible. Like I was pretending it was still just me and Dad. That hadn't been the best thing to do.

When I thought more about it, I felt bad that they had

tried to help, and I had turned them down. Was it too late? Could they still get me out of this terrible mess?

I would have to ask them. I decided to rest for a few more minutes, and then actually ask my new family for help. My eyes burned from crying, and I closed them. I felt my charm hanging on a chain around my neck, and I held it tightly with both hands.

(All of us Disney Girls have special charms. I have a tiny real crystal slipper that my dad gave me long ago. Yukiko has a small gold heart. Paula's is a silver feather. Isabelle's is a tiny silver mirror. Jasmine has a gold lamp that she often wears as a bracelet. And Ariel has a gold seashell, of course.) We use them to make magic wishes, or anytime we need extra help. I figured this situation definitely qualified!

As I felt my charm grow warm inside my hands, I made a wish:

All the magic powers that be,
Hear me now, my special plea.
It's Cinderella, in a mess.
Please help my castle be the best.

There. I still didn't know how I would get out of this disaster, but with magic and my new family on my side, I could give it a try.

With my eyes still closed, I pictured myself proudly carrying in the gingerbread castle of my dreams. Ms. Timmons made a space for me to set it down on the party table. My classmates gathered around, oohing and aahing. My fellow DGs gave me proud, happy glances. I felt like a real princess.

I sighed, feeling myself relax into my pillow. That would be so incredible. It would be a dream come true. . . .

Chapter Fourteen

A Dream Come True

Eight o'clock: The Princess finally arises . . . what?!

My eyes popped open to the sound of hungry squeak-ing coming from Jaq and Gus's cage. Bright winter sun-light filled my room. What time was it? Eight o'clock! I was half an hour late! I leaped out of bed as if electrified, threw some food to Jaq and Gus, and raced to my closet.

I stopped dead before I threw open the closet door. Oh, my gosh! Today was Friday. A horrible, sickening feeling grabbed my stomach and gave it a sharp twist. Today was the class holiday party! I cast my mind back to the night before, remembering the Disney Girls' food fight, Alana sending them home, and myself deciding to rest for a few minutes before I worked on the castle again . . .

I looked down at myself. I was still wearing my comfy sweats. I had never gotten up! I had never worked on the castle again! I was doomed. Doomed!

I sank to my knees in front of my closet, groaning.

A quick tap on my door, then Lucy stuck her head in.

"I know," I said glumly. "I'm late."

"Yep," said Lucy. "Hurry up." The door closed again.

Without bothering to dress, I thudded my way downstairs, already trying to think up a convincing illness. I rubbed my throat. Was it scratchy? My stomach really *did* hurt. Maybe it was appendicitis. . . .

I plodded into the kitchen, my head hanging low. Instead of the usual breakfast sounds, it was silent. I raised my head and saw my family seated around the kitchen table, grinning at me. I guess they thought the complete and total destruction of my life was funny.

Then I saw it. My jaw dropped open.

On the kitchen counter stood an incredible, fabulous gingerbread castle! I stared at it, wondering if I were still dreaming. I looked from it to my smiling family, but my brain just would not compute.

"Wha—?" I whispered. I floated over to examine the castle more closely. It had four walls, a drawbridge, and four towers topped with upside-down ice-cream cones decorated to look like turrets. Icing icicles dripped from every edge. The roof was scalloped with more icing to look like tiles. There were clear, colored windows made from melted hard candies. Green coconut grass surrounded the castle, and the chocolate-kiss tree was propped in the yard in a ball of modeling clay. Each window was bordered with peppermint sticks and topped by a row of red-hot candies. Tiny silver candy balls were sprinkled everywhere. Peppermint canes made a striped fence up the drawbridge, which was made by a bar of white chocolate. Finally, a cloud of spun sugar formed smoke over the fireplace, which had been made by sticking rock candy to the wall of the castle.

It was totally, totally awesome and magical.

Wait a minute. Magical? My eyes widened. Had the magic done this? Or . . . had my family?

"I don't believe this, you guys," I stammered, overwhelmed. "This is incredible. You all must have been up all night."

My dad shook his head. "No, honey. We just found this here when we got up this morning. Didn't you make it?"

I squinted at him. "No, of course not," I said. "I fell asleep. You all must have made it." Unless it was magic.

Lucy and Jane shook their heads. "Uh-uh," they said. "Not us." Alana looked mystified. I didn't know what to think.

"I better get my stuff," said Lucy. "Don't want to be late." She patted my back on her way out. "Great castle, kid."

"Thank you," I said, bemused.

As she went past, I thought I saw a tiny drop of white icing in her hair. I blinked. She was gone. Had it been there?

"Hurry up and eat," said Alana. "Your dad will give you a ride today, with the castle."

"Okay," I said. I happened to glance at the trash can, and saw a piece of paper sticking out. When I pulled it out, I realized it was a computer blowup of Mr. Pinto's castle drawing. Jane must have done this, late last night. Hadn't she? I watched my dad as I ate breakfast. He looked really tired this morning. So did Alana.

By now I was sure that my family had made my fantabulous gingerbread castle—a castle even better than the one I had dreamed of. And I was equally sure that magic had helped them do it. Anyone looking at the castle could see that magic had been involved.

I wolfed down my breakfast and raced upstairs to get dressed. I was completely off schedule this morning, but since Dad was giving me a ride, I wouldn't be late. Gleefully I pictured everyone's faces as I walked into Ms. Timmons's class, carrying that amazing creation.

I rushed into my room and headed for my closet. Then I had my second magical surprise of the day. Someone had made my bed for me this morning. And spread on the perfectly smooth comforter was a new holiday outfit. And you may not believe this, but it was the *exact* same outfit I had imagined weeks ago—the one my fairy godmother created for me in my dream!

Quickly I put on the pleated, red-plaid kilt. It fit perfectly. The fluffy green sweater looked terrific with it. I pulled on thick red tights and some low, black suede boots. I brushed my hair, and examined the final image in the mirror.

I looked incredibly glossy. I looked like a princess. I looked like *me*.

A tap on my door made me look up. Lucy poked her head in. I remembered what she had said before about my lame clothes. I smiled at her. "Better?" I asked.

"Fabulous," she said, smiling back.

After she left, I held my charm in one hand. "Thank you, magic," I whispered. "Thank you for your help, and thank you for my new family."

"Goodness gracious, Ella," Ms. Timmons said, holding the classroom door open for me. Dad was helping me carry the castle in. It was enormous and heavy. "That's the most beautiful thing I've ever seen. Did you make that yourself?"

"I had a lot of help," I said, grinning at my dad. He grinned back.

Ariel ran up. "Ella!" she said, giving me a hug. "You look so cool and so hot, all at the same time!"

"Thanks," I said.

Yukiko raced up. She stared at the castle, and at me. She nodded knowingly.

"Magic?" she whispered.

"Magic, Mr. Pinto's drawing, your mother's cake-decorating kit, Mrs. Beaumont's recipe, and my family," I whispered back. I kissed my dad good-bye, and thanked him again.

Everyone in my class crowded around the table to see the castle. They oohed and aahed, just like in my fantasy.

I was so proud, but it wasn't for myself. I was proud for my family, my friends, and for magic.

Then Yukiko handed me a glass of punch, Ariel put on some terrific dance music, and I grabbed an almond cookie.

"Let the party begin!" Ariel cried.

As I caught sight of my twirling skirt in one of classroom windows, I knew that no princess ever had it as good as I did, right then.

My heart was pounding as I hunkered down in the azalea bushes. Daisy's little armadillo nose poked through the bars of the cat carrier. I put my finger to my lips, but I didn't really have to worry about her making noise. That was the last thing I had to worry about.

Across my backyard, Isabelle was standing watch behind Dad's lawn chair. From her position, she could see through our kitchen window. She was waiting for my mom to come into the kitchen. My muscles were so tense I felt like a big rubber band, twisted into knots. I could hear Daisy scrabbling in the carrier. She didn't know what was going on. "It's okay, Daisy," I whispered. "This is for your own good."

Isabelle suddenly whirled and signaled me. I gulped. Here we go. Step three of Operation Daisy. Quickly and silently I grabbed Daisy's carrier and slunk to the back of my house. If Mom was in the kitchen, it meant she couldn't hear me open the back door and slither down the hall to my bedroom.

Holding my breath, I slipped inside. It felt mondo weird to be sneaking back *into* my own house. Drawing on my own magical powers of silence and stealth, I snuck into my room. Then I eased open my closet door, shoved a surprised Daisy all the way to the back, and hid her carrier with a pile of soccer equipment.

I didn't take a breath till I had flitted out the back door and raced across the yard. Then I collapsed next to Isabelle, panting and shaking with nerves.

"Mission accomplished," I gasped. "Daisy's back inside."

Isabelle shook her head. "Now all you have to do is keep your parents from finding her."

I gulped in air. My stomach sank. If my parents found my pet armadillo, I would be in *biiiig* trouble.

Read all the books in the
Disney Girls series!

#1 One of Us

Jasmine is thrilled to be a Disney Girl. It means she has four best friends—Ariel, Yukiko, Paula, and Ella. But she still doesn't have a *best,* best friend. Then she meets Isabelle Beaumont, the new girl. Maybe Isabelle could be Jasmine's *best* best friend—but could she be a *Disney Girl?*

#2 Attack of the Beast: Isabelle's Story

Isabelle's next-door neighbor Kenny has been a total Beast for as long as she can remember. But now he's gone too far: he secretly videotaped the Disney Girls singing and dancing and acting silly at Isabelle's slumber party. Isabelle vows to get the tape back, but how will she ever get past the Beast?

#3 And Sleepy Makes Seven

Mrs. Hayashi is expecting a baby soon, and Yukiko is praying that this time it'll be a girl. She's already got six younger brothers and stepbrothers, and this is her last chance for a sister. All of the Disney Girls are hoping that with a little magic, Yukiko's fondest wish will come true.

#4 A Fish Out of Water

Ariel in ballet class? That's like putting a fish in the middle of the desert! Even though Ariel's the star of her swim team, she decides that she wants to spend more time with the other Disney Girls. So she joins Jasmine and Yukiko's ballet class.

But has Ariel made a mistake, or will she trade in her flippers for toe shoes forever?

#5 *Cinderella's Castle*

The Disney Girls are so excited about the school's holiday party. Ella decides that the perfect thing for her to make is an elaborate gingerbread castle. But creating such a complicated confection isn't easy, even for someone as super-organized as Ella. And her stepfamily just doesn't seem to understand how important this is to her. Ella could really use a fairy god-mother right now . . .

#6 *One Pet Too Many*

Paula's always loved animals, any animal. Who else would have a pet raccoon, not to mention two cats, a dog, three rabbits, and countless fish? When Paula finds a lost baby armadillo, though, her parents say, "No more pets!"—and that's that. But how much trouble could a baby armadillo be? Plenty, as Paula discovers—especially when she's trying to keep it a secret from her parents.

#7 *Adventure in Walt Disney World:*
A Disney Girls Super Special

The Disney Girls are so excited. They're all going to dress up as their favorite Disney Princesses and go to the Magic Kingdom. And as a special treat, Jasmine's mom is taking them to stay overnight at a hotel in the park. Magical things are bound to happen to the Disney Girls in the most magical place on earth—and they do . . .